CLA[SSICS RE]TOLD

Jane Eyre

RETOLD BY
MAGGIE PEARSON

ILLUSTRATED BY
PAUL FISHER

LONDON·SYDNEY

First published in 2011 by
Franklin Watts
338 Euston Road
London NW1 3BH

Franklin Watts Australia
Level 17/207 Kent Street
Sydney NSW 2000

A CIP catalogue record for this book
is available from the British Library.

ISBN: 978 1 4451 0462 1

Dewey Classification: 823.9'14

3 5 7 9 10 8 6 4 2

Printed in Great Britain

Franklin Watts is a division of Hachette Children's Books,
an Hachette UK company.
www.hachette.co.uk

Contents

Chapter One
Banished

"Jane Eyre! Where are you?"

Where was I? Locked in the Red Room again, the room where my uncle died and hiding under the bed in fear of his ghost.

My uncle was a kind man, who took me in after my parents died. He treated me like one of his own children. Then he, too, died. His widow hated me and my cousins took their cue from her. The girls were stand-offish and spiteful, and John was a bully who'd hit a girl half his size and run crying to his mother when I hit him back.

That's how I came to be shut in the Red Room again till the maid, Bessie, came in to dry my tears.

"There's someone here to see you, Jane," she told me.

My visitor's name was Mr Brocklehurst. He was tall and broad, and dressed in black.

"Are you a good girl, Jane Eyre?" he asked. I knew if I said yes, my aunt would say no.

"I don't know," I said.

"Do you know where bad little girls go when they die?" he demanded.

"They go to hell, sir."

"And what is hell?"

"It is a pit full of fire."

"And do you want to fall into that pit and burn there for ever?"

"No, sir."

"So what must you do to avoid it?"

"I must stay healthy and not die."

My aunt gave a little cry. "You heard her, Mr Brocklehurst! That child is evil."

Mr Brocklehurst smiled. "At Lowood we will cure her."

So I was to be sent away to school. To Lowood School for Orphan Girls.

I've never been so cold as I was that winter at Lowood. Never so cold, never so hungry, never so frightened of breaking some rule I'd never heard of until it was too late. Even Miss Temple, the principal, was frightened of breaking the rules.

Mr Brocklehurst was the owner of Lowood School. His mother had set up the school many years before, but she would not have been happy to see how Mr Brocklehurst ran the school now.

But it was at Lowood that I made my first true friend. Her name was Helen Burns. She was the sweetest, kindest girl that ever walked this earth. Yet there was one teacher who was always picking on her.

"Why do you take it? Why don't you fight back?" I asked her.

"Because she's right," said Helen. "I do dream in class. I am untidy. She's our teacher. It's her job to correct me."

"You can still hate her," I said. I told her about my aunt and my cousins.

"Do you hate them?" said Helen.

"I do!" I said. "With all my heart and soul!"

"What does that do to your heart and soul, Jane? It makes you bitter and does them no harm at all. Forgive them, Jane, as our Lord Jesus told us to do. Or, if you cannot, put the past behind you. Let it go."

Put the past behind you was easily said, but not so easily done on the day Mr Brocklehurst came to inspect the school.

I kept my head down, but his sharp eyes found me out. "Jane Eyre! Come here."

He stood me on a stool so that everyone could see me.

"Look at her!" thundered Mr Brocklehurst. "She looks just like one of you. But she is a creature of the devil! You must never speak to her. Never play with her! Shut her out!"

Why didn't I stand up for myself?

Because I knew no-one would believe me. So there I stood while all the girls filed out, turning their heads away. Except for Helen, who gave me a little smile.

Afterwards I cried and cried. "The whole world hates me now!" I said to Helen.

"Don't be silly," she said. "There are millions of people in the world. Most of them have never heard of Jane Eyre. And do you think anyone at Lowood cares for what Mr Brocklehurst says or thinks?"

At long last spring came, but it brought the deadly typhus fever with it.

Girl after girl at Lowood fell sick and died. Coffin after coffin was buried in the churchyard.

Helen was sick too, but not with typhus fever.

"Consumption of the lungs," said the doctor, shaking his head.

Helen was hidden away in Miss Temple's room. I was not allowed to see her.

But late one night I crept out of bed and along the corridor. Miss Temple was not there.

Helen was huddled on a cot under some blankets. She was pale and thin, but as she heard me open the door, she opened her eyes and smiled.

"Jane!" she said. "I hoped you'd come. I didn't want to go without saying goodbye."

She was taken over by a violent fit of coughing. When it was over, she lay back.

"But where are you going?" I asked.

"Home," she said. "Home to Jesus. Please don't cry. You should be happy for me."

"But what about me?" I sobbed. "Please don't leave me."

"I won't leave you, Jane. I'll always be with you, for as long as you remember me."

When Miss Temple came in, she found us lying side by side. I was sound asleep and Helen was dead.

Chapter Two
Thornfield Hall

After news of the typhus outbreak got into the papers, we were treated better at Lowood. We had warmer clothes and more to eat. I discovered that I was a good, keen student and began to enjoy my lessons. Eventually, I became a teacher myself.

During that time, Miss Temple and I became close. Indeed, I thought of her less as a teacher and more as a friend. One day, Miss Temple announced that she would be leaving Lowood to be married. The news left me feeling sad and restless, and ready for a change of my own.

I decided to put an advertisement looking for a position as a governess in the local newspaper. I soon had a reply, from a Mrs Fairfax of Thornfield Hall, offering me the job of governess to a girl of seven years old. I decided there and then to take the job.

Within a few days, I was on my way to Thornfield Hall. The journey was long and it was dark when I got there. The great, dark house loomed over me. There was just one light burning in a downstairs room where an elderly lady, Mrs Fairfax, was waiting for me.

She was so kind, so welcoming! She sat me down in front of the fire with a bowl of hot soup and home-baked bread and chattered away about how nice it would be to have another woman there for company, apart from the servants.

"When shall I meet Miss Fairfax?" I asked her.

"Miss Fairfax?" she said. "You mean Miss Adele! She's not mine. She's Mr Rochester's ward, the orphan child of some French friends of his."

"Who is Mr Rochester?"

"The master, of course. I'm just the housekeeper. He's a good master, though he sometimes has strange, black moods. But he's not here at the moment. He seldom is."

Next day I met my new pupil, Adele. She was a pretty little girl and as bright as a button, but easily distracted and not used to lessons. By lunchtime we were both quite worn out. I was glad to give her the afternoon off while Mrs Fairfax showed me around the house. It seemed to go on for ever.

"How many bedrooms are there?" I asked.

"I've never counted," Mrs Fairfax replied. "But we keep them all ready in case Mr Rochester comes home without warning and brings company with him."

She smiled. "I always say that if we had a ghost at Thornfield, they'd at least be comfortable."

"So there are no ghosts?" I asked.

"None that I've ever seen," she said.

As she said that, I heard a strange noise for the first time. The sound of a woman laughing. If you could call it a laugh. It was more like the cry of some animal.

"Did you hear that?" I asked, shaken.

"That's just Grace Poole," she said. "She's one of the servants. An odd sort of creature, keeps herself to herself and sleeps up there in the attic. But there's no harm in her. No harm at all."

Whenever I heard that strange, eerie laughter after that, I told myself it was just Grace Poole. Though it was hard to imagine Grace Poole ever laughing. She was a heavy, no-nonsense sort of woman who, whenever I spoke to her, never looked at me but only nodded and hurried past.

Chapter Three
Mr Rochester

I began to feel as if I'd never lived anywhere else but Thornfield.

Late one winter's afternoon, I was on my way back to the hall after posting a letter in the village. The moon was up, a mist was rising and there were patches of ice on the road. Suddenly a great black-and-white dog came trotting towards me out of the mist.

I stood back to let it pass, which it did, before vanishing again into the mist.

After it came a man on horseback.

He, too, passed me without a glance.

Then the spell was broken.

The horse slipped on a patch of ice. I heard its frightened neigh as it fell. And the man's angry cry as he was thrown from the saddle.

The horse was up again in a moment, but the man lay still on the ground.

I hurried over to him.

"Are you hurt, sir?" I asked him.

"It's just a sprain. I'll live."

"Shall I fetch help?" I said. "I can run down to Thornfield Hall."

"Thornfield Hall?" he said.

"It's where I live. It's not far."

"I know where it is! What are you? A servant?"

"I am the governess there," I said.

"The governess!" He nodded. "Of course. I had forgotten. No need to trouble them. Just pull me up and help me onto my horse."

It was done in a moment. Then horse, rider and dog vanished again into the mist. He was not a young man, or handsome, but his face stayed in my mind as I walked back to the Hall.

Imagine my surprise when I got to Thornfield Hall to find the same black-and-white dog standing in the kitchen. Then in bustled Mrs Fairfax.

"The master's home!" she cried. "He took a tumble on the icy road but the doctor's with him now."

So that was Mr Rochester, I thought to myself.

All Adele could talk of the next day was Mr Rochester. "What present do you think he has brought me?" she kept asking.

She had to wait till that evening before Mr Rochester called us to the drawing room.

There she threw herself into Mr Rochester's arms. "Where is my present?" she demanded.

"All she wants from me is presents!"
Mr Rochester sighed, handing her a large,
beautifully gift-wrapped box.

"And have you
brought a
present for Miss
Eyre?" she
added.

I could see that
surprised him.

"When did you
ever ask for a
present for
anyone but
yourself?" he
asked her.

"Did you expect a present, Miss Eyre?"

"Of course not!" I said. "You do not know
me and I have done nothing to deserve it."

"That's true!" Mr Rochester said. "I have
Miss Eyre to thank for this!" He pointed to
his bandaged ankle. "She put that patch of

ice in my path to make my horse stumble."

"Indeed I did not!" I said.

"No? Mrs Fairfax tells me you are an orphan. But I think you are a fairy. A changeling. I think you were standing there in the mist and the moonlight, waiting for your people to claim you."

I shook my head. "I should have had a long wait, for the fairy folk left these lands centuries ago!"

That was how we began. And that was how we carried on. He was so easy to talk to!

Sometimes I didn't know whether he was serious or joking. But he never made me feel I was anything less than his equal.

So one day when he asked me, "Do you think I'm handsome?"

I replied, "No, sir," without thinking.

Then I added, "But I think a man's true worth lies in his heart and soul."

"And what if his heart and soul are uglier still?" he said.

"I cannot believe that of you, sir."

"No? Oh, Jane, you do not know me! But, if a man has made a mistake when he is young, do you think he should suffer for it his whole life long?"

I said, "I think, if he is truly sorry, God will forgive him."

"But would the world forgive him?"

"I know I would forgive you," I said.

"I think you would," he said.

That was when I knew I was in love with Mr Rochester. Of course he could never love me. I was poor, plain and a governess, hardly better than a servant. But Mrs Fairfax said he had never stayed so long at Thornfield before. She even talked of him settling down. That would have been enough for me. To see him every day and talk to him.

Chapter Four
Fire!

I had grown used to Grace Poole's strange ways by now. The mad bursts of laughter. The footsteps in the middle of the night. Then one night I was woken by that same eerie laughter. It sounded as if it came from right outside my door.

I called out, "Who's there?" She laughed again. Then I heard her moving away along the corridor.

When I looked out I found a candle burning on the floor outside and a smell of smoke. Further along the corridor, the air was black with it.

On I went, to where the smoke was thickest and found the door to Mr Rochester's room standing open.

He was lying asleep on the bed, flames licking upwards all around him.

I cried out, "Mr Rochester! Wake up!"

Then I seized the water jug from the dressing table and emptied it over the bed. After that, I emptied the washing bowl over the flames.

I ran back to my room twice to fetch my own jug and bowl, and flung the water over the smouldering bedclothes.

Mr Rochester woke at last, dazed by the smoke.

"What have you done to me, Jane?" he exclaimed. Then he saw the blackened bedclothes and smelt the smoke.

I told him about the voice I'd heard. The candle left burning outside my door.

"It was Grace Poole," I said. "I know it."

"Leave her to me," he said.

He took both my hands in his.

"You have saved my life, Jane. Promise me you won't speak about this to anyone."

With a heavy heart, I promised.

The next morning the servants' talk was all of how Mr Rochester had been reading in bed and somehow knocked the candle over, setting fire to his bedclothes.

And Grace Poole went about as usual. Why hadn't she been locked up? Why didn't Mr Rochester send her away? What hold did she have over him? I asked myself.

Mr Rochester himself was not there to ask. He'd left the house straight after breakfast to visit some people called Ingram who lived not far away.

At the name of Ingram, Mrs Fairfax looked knowing and talked again of Mr Rochester settling down. Miss Ingram was such a beauty! So elegant! So talented! On and on she chattered.

I was heartily sick of Blanche Ingram before I ever set eyes on her, which was three long weeks later when Mr Rochester came home and brought the whole Ingram family with him.

Yes, Miss Blanche Ingram was very beautiful. She was also vain and shallow and selfish, and rude to poor little Adele.

When Mr Rochester asked me what I thought of Miss Ingram, the best I could say was, "She is very beautiful."

He asked, "Do you think I should marry her?"

I replied, "If she will make you happy."

He said, "Why would she marry me, Jane? Not for my looks!"

"Perhaps she sees beyond your looks."

"She sees my money!" he said bitterly.

Yet everyone was sure he would marry her.

The Ingrams stayed on. There was music and dancing every evening. I sat in a corner and longed to be back in my room.

Then one evening a visitor arrived, a Mr Mason, from Jamaica.

I saw Mr Rochester turn pale at the sound of his name, though Mr Mason seemed very ordinary when he was brought to meet us.

That night I was woken by a terrible scream. The scream of a man in terror and agony.

"Rochester! Help me!"

I found everyone gathered on the landing.
"A servant has had a bad dream," Mr
Rochester told them. "Go back to bed."

To me he said quietly, "Go back to your
room and wait for me. I need your help."

The house was quiet again when Mr
Rochester came for me. He led me to a door
where I had seen Grace Poole going in and
out. Then up a flight of stairs to a room in
the attic where Mr Mason lay with a gaping
wound in his chest.

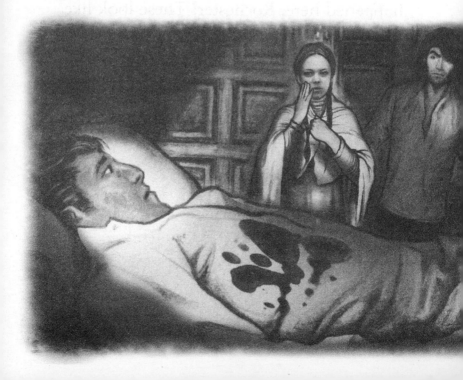

"Look after him while I fetch the doctor," said Mr Rochester.

I did what I could to make Mr Mason comfortable. Then I waited. The night seemed endless. From behind a door on the other side of the room came that same eerie laughter and sounds like an animal dragging itself across the floor.

At last Mr Rochester came, with the doctor, who took one look at the wound and exclaimed, "In God's name, what has happened here, Rochester? These look like teeth marks."

"Just do your job," said Mr Rochester. "I want him out of here before morning."

Together we helped Mr Mason downstairs. As we helped him into the doctor's carriage Mr Mason whispered, "Take care of her, Rochester."

Mr Rochester looked at him grimly. "You have my word."

I thought it strange that both of them should be so concerned for a woman like Grace Poole.

Chapter Five
A wedding

After the Ingrams left, all Mrs Fairfax could talk of was weddings.

A new carriage arrived for the new Mrs Rochester. The family jewels were sent for from London. And there was talk of sending Adele away to school.

"So I must look for a new job," I said.

"I have friends in Ireland who are looking for a governess," said Mr Rochester.

"In Ireland?" I said. "I can't go to Ireland."

"Why not?" he demanded, a gentle smile playing about his lips.

My eyes filled with tears. "Because I would never see you – I mean Thornfield – again!"

"Then stay here, Jane."

"I can't stay here! Not once you are married. I couldn't bear it."

"Who would I marry, Jane?"

"Blanche Ingram of course!"

"Blanche Ingram?" He laughed. "You think I am going to marry Blanche Ingram?"

"But who else is there?"

"You, Jane."

I said, "Please don't make fun of me, sir. You think that because I am poor and plain and you pay me thirty pounds a year that I have no feelings?"

He shook his head. "I'm not making fun of you, Jane. I'm asking you to be my wife."

It was true. I was to become Mrs Rochester.

My eyes filled once more, but this time with tears of happiness.

I should have dreamed sweet dreams that night. Instead, I dreamed that Thornfield Hall was a blackened ruin. Birds nested in the roofless eaves. Weeds grew among the flagstones in the hall. And I wandered there all alone.

There was a storm that night. Adele told me over breakfast that the great chestnut tree in the park had been split in two by lightning. I decided that it was the storm that had given me such dark dreams.

And Mr Rochester said that we must be married within a month! The time flew by.

The night before my wedding I had another bad dream. Or was it just a dream?

I woke to find someone in my room. It was a woman, but not Mrs Fairfax, nor any of the servants, nor even Grace Poole. I saw her face in the mirror and I knew that this was the creature that had almost killed Mr Mason.

I must have fainted, for the next thing I knew, it was morning. The morning of my wedding day. And there on the bed lay my wedding veil, torn in two!

"What do you need a veil for?" said Mr Rochester. "There'll be no-one there to see you except me and the vicar and the two witnesses."

I'd asked for a quiet wedding and a very quiet wedding it was. Not even Mrs Fairfax and Adele were invited.

The vicar began, "If any man knows of any reason why these two should not be joined in marriage-"

A voice spoke from the back of the church. "I do!"

It was Mr Mason.

"Mr Rochester is already married," he said. "To my sister, Bertha Mason! I have the marriage document here in my hand!"

Mr Rochester stormed towards him, but stopped himself. Instead, he seized me by the wrist and dragged me back to the house, Mr Mason following. Up to that attic room we climbed, where I'd nursed Mr Mason through that long, long night. There sat Grace Poole quietly knitting.

"How is your patient today, Mrs Poole?" said Mr Rochester.

"Fair to middling, sir."

"Let me see."

She unlocked a door on the far side.

In a corner of the room crouched the foul creature I'd seen in my room. Suddenly I understood that this madwoman was behind all the fear and menace at Thornfield.

"That is my wife! She was beautiful once," said Mr Rochester. "The signs of madness had hardly begun to show. I was in love. I was dazzled! But your family knew what she was, Mason, when they married her to me."

"Now I am tied to her till death do us part! I ask you, Jane! Is that right? Is that fair?"

I could not answer him. Mr Rochester said that he loved me, but he had tried to trick me into a marriage that was no kind of marriage at all.

Then the creature flung herself at him, teeth bared, nails like claws. I think he would have let her tear him limb from limb if Grace Poole had not dragged her away.

"You'd best leave now," she said.

Chapter Six
Farewell to Thornfield

I left Thornfield early the next morning.
I took the first coach out of the village.

"Where to, miss?" said the driver.

"As far as this will take me," I said, giving
him all the money I had.

He took me at my word and set me down
at a crossroads without so much as a
signpost to point me to the nearest village.
From there I walked, not caring if I lived or
died.

Yet, when I found berries I ate them.
When I found water, I drank. I slept out
under the stars. I grew weaker by the day,
but at last I came to a village where a kindly
clergyman, Mr Rivers, and his sisters took
me in.

They nursed me and, when I was well
again, they found me a job in the village
school.

I had a new life, with friends who cared for me. But every night I dreamed of Thornfield Hall and every day I thought of Mr Rochester.

Then one day, in my head, I heard his voice calling "Jane! Jane! Jane!" He sounded so lost, so alone, so frightened. I took the very next coach back to Thornfield.

I found it a blackened ruin, just as I'd seen in my dream.

"It was the madwoman," someone told me in the village. "The madwoman he kept locked in the attic. Seems she got out one night and set fire to the place!"

Another villager went on, "All the servants were safe and Mr Rochester, too. But he went back in to save her. She was dancing about the roof. He begged her to come down. But then she jumped."

"Is she dead?" I asked.

"Aye. Dashed her brains out on the courtyard cobblestones."

"And Mr Rochester?" I asked, fearfully.

"They got him out."

"He's still alive?"

"If you can call it living. His left hand was crushed as the building fell. And he's stone blind into the bargain."

I found Mr Rochester living in a house deep in the forest with only two old servants to care for him.

He'd asked for a glass of water. I told them I would take it to him.

My hand trembled so much that most of the water was spilt on the floor.

"I'm sorry," I said. "I'll pour some more."

"Jane?" he said. "Is that Jane Eyre? It can't be! I must be dreaming."

"If you are," I said, "then so am I."

"My dream – your nightmare," he said. "This is the man you would have married. A one-armed cripple who can't see!"

"This is the man I will marry," I said. "If he'll have me."

"I don't want your pity!"

"You won't get it," I said. "Only my love."

So, reader, I married him.

That was ten years ago. We live quietly and we are happy. Adele goes to school close by and we see her often.

We are happier still since the day when he suddenly said to me, "Jane! Are you wearing something bright around your neck?"

It was a gold necklace.

"Yes," I replied.

"And are you wearing a blue dress?"

"Yes!'

He still cannot see well enough to read or write, but he can get about now without me to lead him. And when he held our first-born son in his arms he could see that the baby had his eyes.

Charlotte Brontë (1816–1855)

Charlotte Brontë was born on 21 April 1816 in Yorkshire. Her early years were marked with tragedy, as she lost not only her two older sisters, but also her mother while she was still young.

Charlotte and her two surviving sisters, Anne and Emily, and their brother Branwell, were mostly taught at home. They were all creative and began writing stories and poems about imaginary lands at an early age.

Charlotte Brontë

In 1846 the three Brontë sisters published a book of poetry under the pseudonyms Currer, Acton and Ellis Bell. The poems were not well received, and the book only sold

two copies, but undeterred, each of the sisters went on to write novels that are now considered classics. In 1847 Charlotte's novel *Jane Eyre* and Anne's *Agnes Grey* were both published. In 1848, Emily's only book, *Wuthering Heights*, appeared.

Tragically, all of the sisters' lives were cut short by illness. Anne and Emily both died of tuberculosis within six months of each other. Charlotte lived long enough to become a celebrated literary figure, but died of tuberculosis in 1855, aged just 38.

Jane Eyre (1847)

Jane Eyre draws a lot upon Charlotte's own life. She briefly attended a boarding school much like Lowood, and worked at times as a governess to support her family. She also lost beloved family members to tuberculosis, just as Jane loses her friend Helen. Charlotte was also a strong character, who overcame much hardship in her life, just like Jane.

Titles in the CLASSICS RETOLD series:

978 1 4451 0461 4
eBook edition: 978 1 4451 0818 6

978 1 4451 0460 7
eBook edition: 978 1 4451 0815 5

978 1 4451 0458 4
eBook edition: 978 1 4451 0819 3

978 1 4451 0462 1
eBook edition: 978 1 4451 0817 9

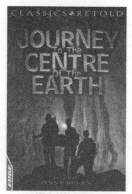

978 1 4451 0459 1
eBook edition: 978 1 4451 0816 2

978 1 4451 0457 7
eBook edition: 978 1 4451 0820 9